SIM
4a

Mon

D1079838

# Monkey Talk

## Written by Moya Simons
## Illustrated by Mitch Vane

Travelling Book Fair

2003

Commission Order

An easy-to-read SOLO
for beginning readers

SOLOS

This book has been withdrawn from James Gillespie's Primary School library

JAMES GILLESPIES
PRIMARY SCHOOL
WHITEHOUSE LOAN
EDINBURGH
EH9 1BD

Southwood Books Limited
4 Southwood Lawn Road
London N6 5SF

First published in Australia by Omnibus Books 1999

Published in the UK under licence from
Omnibus Books by
Southwood Books Limited, 2001

Reprinted 2001 (twice)

Text copyright © Moya Simons 1999
Illustrations copyright © Mitch Vane 1999

Cover design by Lyn Mitchell

ISBN 1 903207 29 0

Printed in Hong Kong

A CIP catalogue record for this book is available
from the British Library

All rights reserved. No part of this publication may be
reproduced, stored in or introduced into a retrieval system,
or transmitted in any form or by any means, (electronic,
mechanical, photocopying, recording or otherwise), without
the prior written permission of both the copyright holder
and the publisher.

*For Tamie and Suzy, with love – M.S.*

*For Becky, Steve, Kate and Jessica – M.V.*

## Chapter 1

Bub Tub was two-and-a-bit years old. She thought her big brother Danny was wonderful.

Bub Tub's real name was Penny, but Danny called her Bub Tub. He said, "It's a good name for you, because you're a baby and you dribble enough to fill a bath tub."

Bub Tub blew her best dribble bubble when Danny told her that.

Bub Tub wanted to be just like
Danny. Danny could ride a bike.
Bub Tub could only waddle around
like a duck.

Danny could climb trees, too. Once he'd climbed the tree outside her bedroom window to get a better look at the moon.

But what Bub Tub liked best about Danny was that every time he spoke, everyone understood exactly what he meant.

Bub Tub knew what she wanted to say, but when the words came out they sounded something like this: "Iggle bug da doody. Da doom. Ba boody."

This could mean "I think those ants would make a nice dinner" or "I need to go to the toilet in a hurry."

## Chapter 2

"Isn't it time Penny began to talk?"
Bub Tub's mum said one day. "She
should be speaking in sentences by
now. She only says the odd word
here and there."

"Don't worry," said Dad. "Sooner or later she'll be able to talk properly."

"Ga boom," agreed Bub Tub.

Dad looked at her and scratched his head. He had no idea what Bub Tub was saying.

## Chapter 3

One Sunday afternoon the family went to the zoo. First they went to see the monkeys.

"I love monkeys," said Danny. "Do you like monkeys, Bub Tub?"

"Ga floofy, iggle bug," Bub Tub said. Then she felt sad because she knew Danny hadn't understood a word. He probably thought she'd never learn to speak like other kids.

Bub Tub, Danny, Mum and Dad stopped to look at the monkeys.

The monkeys were swinging on
branches or sitting on the grass
chattering. Some had fleas and
were busy scratching themselves
and each other.

Bub Tub held tightly to Mum's hand. She listened to everyone talking around her. She understood everything they said.

She listened to the monkeys. She understood what they were saying too.

That monkey sitting in the tree was saying to his friend, "You pinched my peanuts. If you do that again I'll dong you on the head."

## Chapter 4

Bub Tub couldn't see over the wall.
Mum reached down to lift her up.

Bub Tub turned and squirmed.
She wriggled and dribbled.

She didn't want to be picked up.
She just wanted to be taller.

Mum was holding a brown paper bag full of sandwiches in one arm, and Bub Tub in the other arm. Bub Tub was so wriggly that Mum lost her balance.

Bub Tub wobbled and fell.

Dad reached out to grab Bub Tub but grabbed the brown paper bag instead.

Danny reached out to grab Bub Tub but ended up grabbing a cheese sandwich.

Bub Tub toppled over the railing. She looked like a round, fat, pink ball.

She landed on soft grass on the other side.

## Chapter 5

Mum screamed. Dad screamed. Danny had a bite of the cheese sandwich, then he screamed.

People gathered around. They screamed too.

Someone ran to get a zoo keeper.

Two big monkeys sat down beside
Bub Tub on the grass.

Danny frowned. He wondered
what the monkeys would do to her
when she dribbled on them.

"Da doody," said Bub Tub to one monkey. "Ah flum. Ga boody."

The monkey leaned over, checked her out for fleas, then chattered back. He understood every word she said.

He offered her a banana. Bub Tub said, "Ta." He didn't understand that, so she added, "Ga blob."

He flashed a toothy monkey smile at her.

Bub Tub munched on the banana.

Then she cuddled up to the monkeys while they screeched questions at her.

"Are the people here to watch us, or are we here to watch them?" they asked.

"Ga blu," Bub Tub said. This meant "I think everyone's here to watch each other."

The monkeys nodded their heads. A few other monkeys climbed down from the trees and sat beside Bub Tub.

"What are those other animal noises we hear?" asked one monkey, who had a very large pink bottom.

Bub Tub said, "Ga flu. Iffle ha da doody." This meant "Lions and tigers and elephants make those noises."

A few monkeys shrieked at that.

"What kind of monkey are you?" asked another monkey.

"Iffle uffle Bub Tub," said Bub Tub.

"She's a Bub Tub monkey," explained a monkey with a wise face and a very, very large pink bottom.

Then they all had a go at running
their furry fingers through Bub Tub's
fair hair.

"No fleas," said one. "That's a
shame."

## Chapter 6

Dad, red-faced and nervous, had climbed over the wall. He was still holding the brown paper bag.

He shook it at the monkeys.
"Go. Shoo," he said.

"Uffle iggle doddle ig," said Bub Tub sadly.

"Yes, it's a shame, but if he's your dad I guess we should do as he says. We'll just climb back into the trees," said the monkeys.

And they did.

A zoo keeper arrived.
"Save my baby," screamed Mum.

Dad and the zoo keeper grabbed Bub Tub while the monkeys chattered in the trees around them. Everyone cheered.

The zoo keeper let Dad and Bub Tub out through a side door.

Bub Tub waved to the monkeys and said, "Bye-bye." When they didn't seem to understand, she yelled, "Uffle fliggle."

They all waved back right away.
"Wow, Bub Tub," said Danny.
"You can talk to the monkeys. Let's
go and talk to the lions now."

## Chapter 7

So, though Mum felt faint and Dad
felt sick, they went to see the lions.

The lions were stretched out in the sun. Bub Tub watched them carefully, then called out, "Uddle diddle."

The lions roared back at her.

They came over to the edge of their cage, lifted up their paws and growled at her, "What kind of lion cub are you?"

"Iffle uffle Bub Tub," Bub Tub replied.

Danny whispered to Mum and Dad, "See the way they're answering her? It's amazing!"

Later, when they were leaving the
zoo, Danny looked at Bub Tub and
said, "Don't worry if you can't talk
like me for a while, Bub Tub. You
can speak monkey talk and lion
talk. I bet you even know a bit of
zebra. You're a smart kid."

Bub Tub blew a big dribble bubble and smiled. She knew that one day she'd talk just like Danny.

She'd do all kinds of things. Maybe she'd even climb the tree outside her bedroom window to have a closer look at the moon.

Until then, if she wanted to have a chat, Danny could always take her to visit her friends in the zoo.

**Moya Simons**

My daughter Suzy was seven years old when her sister Tamie was born.

Tamie's first word was not "Mummy" or "Daddy", but "Thoosie". From the time she could walk she followed Suzy around the house. She wanted to be just like her big sister.

One day at dinner time Tamie said something that sounded like "Iffle flug, da doody uggle flug, Thoosie." Suzy had no idea what she was trying to say and this made Tamie sad.

That was a long time ago. Now Tamie talks non-stop, and everyone understands her perfectly!

**Mitch Vane**

Bub Tub reminds me of my son Jordie, who is about the same age. He adores his older sister Talia, who is five, and follows her all over the place on his chubby little legs, talking and dribbling. He gets very cross and yells when we can't understand what he is trying to say.

I used Jordie as a model when I was drawing Bub Tub for this book, but it was hard because he would never stay still for very long.

I really enjoyed drawing the monkeys. They are like cheeky little children, and just as cute!

# More Solos!

**Dog Star**
Janeen Brian and Ann James

**The Best Pet**
Penny Matthews and Beth Norling

**Fuzz the Famous Fly**
Emily Rodda and Tom Jellett

**Cat Chocolate**
Kate Darling and Mitch Vane

**Green Fingers**
Emily Rodda and Craig Smith

**Gabby's Fair**
Robin Klein and Michael Johnson

**Watch Out William**
Nette Hilton and Beth Norling

**The Great Jimbo James**
Phil Cummings and David Cox